PoKé

I want to be the very b
To beat all the rest, ye

Catch 'em, Catch 'em, Gotta ea

Pokémon I'll search across the land
Look far and wide
Release from my hand
The power that's inside

Catch 'em, Catch 'em, Gotta catch 'em all
Pokémon!

Gotta catch 'em all, Gotta catch 'em all
Gotta catch 'em all, Gotta catch 'em all

At least one hundred and fifty or more to see
To be a Pokémon Master is my destiny

Catch 'em, Catch 'em, Ggotta catch 'em all
Gotta catch 'em all, Pokémon!

Catch 'em, Catch 'em, Gotta catch 'em all
Gotta catch 'em all, Pokémon!

Catch 'em, Catch 'em, Gotta catch 'em all
Gotta catch 'em all, Pokémon!

Can YOU Rap all 150?
Here's the first 32 Pokémon.
Check out Chapter Book #6
Charizard, Go!
for more of the Poké Rap.

Electrode, Diglett, Nidoran, Mankey
Venusaur, Rattata, Fearow, Pidgey
Seaking, Jolteon, Dragonite, Gastly
Ponyta, Vaporeon, Poliwrath, Butterfree

Venomoth, Poliwag, Nidorino, Golduck
Ivysaur, Grimer, Victreebel, Moltres
Nidoking, Farfetch'd, Abra, Jigglypuff
Kingler, Rhyhorn, Clefable, Wigglytuff

Words and Music by Tamara Loeffler and John Siegler
Copyright © 1999 by Pikachu Music (BMI)
Worldwide rights for Pikachu Music administered by Cherry River Music Co. (BMI)
All Rights Reserved   Used By Permission

There are more books
about Pokémon.

Collect them all!

Pokémon™

Team Rocket
Blasts off!

Adapted by Tracey West

SCHOLASTIC INC.
New York   Toronto   London   Auckland   Sydney
Mexico City   New Delhi   Hong Kong

ISBN 0-439-15418-9

©1995, 1996, 1998 Nintendo, CREATURES, GAME FREAK.
TM & ® are trademarks of Nintendo.
© 2000 Nintendo.

All rights reserved. Published by Scholastic Inc.
SCHOLASTIC and associated logos are trademarks
and/or registered trademarks of Scholastic Inc.

12   11   10   9   8   7   6   0   1   2   3   4   5   6/0

Printed in the U.S.A.

First Scholastic printing, January 2000

The World of Pokémon

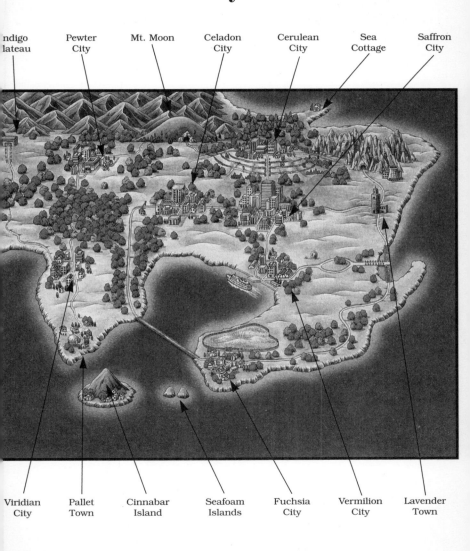

ndigo
lateau

Pewter
City

Mt. Moon

Celadon
City

Cerulean
City

Sea
Cottage

Saffron
City

Viridian
City

Pallet
Town

Cinnabar
Island

Seafoam
Islands

Fuchsia
City

Vermilion
City

Lavender
Town

Spies and Surprises

There are two kinds of people in the world.

People who battle to catch wild Pokémon and work hard to raise them well.

And people who try to steal Pokémon without working hard at all.

Of all the Pokémon thieves in the world, the members of Team Rocket were the worst.

Jessie had a mean streak as long as her red hair.

James was pure trouble — and proud of it.

And their Pokémon, Meowth, was the perfect pal for a pair of Pokémon poachers.

Team Rocket searched the world for rare Pokémon to steal. They wanted to capture one of these amazing creatures to take back to their boss, Giovanni.

But there was one Pokémon they wanted to steal more than any other: Pikachu — an electric Pokémon that looked like a yellow mouse.

Pikachu had shocking powers.

Of course, there were thousands of Pikachu in the world, but there was only one Team Rocket wanted: the Pikachu that belonged to Ash Ketchum, a Pokémon trainer.

Team Rocket knew Ash's Pikachu was special. They were determined to do anything they could to steal the lightning mouse.

Their quest to steal Pikachu led them to Viridian City. Once there, they spied on Ash and his friends from the top of an office building.

"What is that little twerp up to now?" James said. He peered through binoculars.

Jessie snatched the binoculars from his hands. "Let me look," she said. "You can't do anything right."

Meowth, a white Pokémon that looked like a cat, shook its head at both of them. "Be quiet, you two," Meowth said. "We just might find out a thing or two."

Ash and Pikachu stood on the street below, in front of the Viridian City Gym. Ash was talking to his friends Misty and Brock. Misty held a tiny Pokémon in her arms called Togepi. This baby Pokémon hatched from an egg that Ash had found. The bottom of the eggshell was still attached to its body. Tiny arms and legs stuck out from the shell.

Ash stared up at the gym. Tall, white columns led up to the gym doors. The gym's white marble walls gleamed in the afternoon sunlight.

"If I battle the Gym Leader in this gym, I can earn an Earth Badge," Ash said excitedly. "As a Pokémon trainer, I need all the badges I can get!"

"Are you sure you can do it?" Misty asked. "I hear the Gym Leader here is pretty tough!"

Pikachu stood at Ash's side. "*Pika! Pika pika pi!*" Pikachu said.

Ash understood Pikachu's language. "Pikachu says I can do it!" Ash said.

"Well, you *have* learned a lot since you began your journey as a Pokémon trainer," Brock admitted. "I think Pikachu's right."

Ash bent down to Pikachu. "With a pal like you behind me, how can I lose?"

Up on the roof, Jessie rolled her eyes. "That's so sweet, I think I'm going to be sick."

"I may lose my lunch," James said.

"Me too," added Meowth. "Except we

didn't have any lunch today, remember? We're broke again."

Jessie's stomach rumbled. "Don't remind me. We need to bring the Boss a rare Pokémon soon if we want another paycheck."

"Maybe we should just swoop down and grab Pikachu," James suggested.

"*Meowth!* Someone's coming!" Meowth pointed to the sidewalk below.

A shiny red convertible zoomed down the street. A tall boy with wavy brown hair sat in the backseat. A group of cheerleaders sat in the car around him, cheering and waving pom-poms.

"*Gary! Gary! He's the best! Gary! Gary! Beats the rest!*"

Gary stepped out of the car. He swaggered up to the gym doors and faced Ash.

"Still playing with your cute little Poké pals, Ash?" Gary asked snidely.

Ash blushed a little and put Pikachu down on the ground.

"I thought you finally gave up catching and training Pokémon," Gary continued. "I figured you went back home. But it looks like you're still at it. Don't you know when to quit?"

Ash clenched his fists. "You'd better *quit* bugging me," he said angrily. "Or —"

"Or what?" Gary shot back.

Brock pulled Ash back.

"Not now Ash," Brock said. "You're here to get your Earth Badge, remember?"

"That's what you think," Gary said. "They only let *real* Pokémon trainers battle at this gym."

Gary spun around and knocked on the large white doors. The doors swung open, revealing two guards dressed in helmets and bronze breastplates, like ancient Romans.

"I'm Gary from Pallet Town and I hereby request a battle with the leader of this gym," Gary said.

The guards nodded and stepped aside. Gary walked through the doors. His cheerleaders followed.

"See you later, loser!" Gary jeered, then disappeared inside the gym.

Ash grabbed Pikachu and ran up to the guards. "I request a battle, too."

The guards blocked Ash's way.

"Only one trainer allowed in the gym at a time," one of the guards said gruffly.

"But I have to get in!" Ash pleaded. "I need to get an Earth Badge."

"That's the rule," said the other guard.

The heavy doors swung shut in Ash's face.

Ash sank to the stairs. "If I don't do something fast, Gary's going to get way ahead of me!"

Misty shook her head. "Reality check, Ash," she said. "Gary's been way ahead of you from the start!"

Ash groaned and covered his face with his hands.

"Maybe you could go a little easy on Ash right now," Brock told Misty.

"I'm just telling the truth." Misty sighed.

Togepi jumped out of Misty's arms. The tiny Pokémon crawled onto Ash's lap and tapped Ash gently on his shoulder.

Ash thought it was Pikachu. "Oh, Pikachu," Ash said. "You're the only one who stands by me, no matter what."

Ash took his hands away from his face — and saw Togepi.

Startled,
Ash jumped
to his feet,
and Togepi
went flying.
A wild Fearow,
a Flying Pokémon,
was yawning on a nearby ledge.
Togepi landed in Fearow's big beak!

"Togepi! No!" Misty cried.

Fearow flew away from the gym — and toward Team Rocket's secret spying place.

James leaned over the roof with his binoculars.

"What's happening?" Jessie asked. "What's all the commotion?"

"I'm not sure," James said. "It's all happening so — *ouch!*"

The Fearow dropped Togepi from its mouth. Togepi fell on James's head and bounced safely onto the roof.

James stared at the Pokémon in disbelief.

"It's raining rare Pokémon!" Meowth said.

"It's not Pikachu," James said. "But it's the next best thing."

Jessie's gray eyes gleamed greedily. She reached for Togepi.

"Nice Togepi," she said sweetly. "Our Boss will love to meet you!"

2

A Present for the Boss

"*Togi! Togi!*" Togepi hopped out of Jessie's grasp.

The tiny Pokémon toddled along the roof. At the roof's edge, a thin wooden plank led to the roof on the next building. Below the plank was a thirty-foot drop to the street.

Togepi headed right for the plank.

"Stop that Pokémon!" Jessie cried.

It was too late. Togepi stepped onto the narrow plank and began to walk to the next roof.

"Togepi, no! Stop!" Jessie called out.

"*Togi!*" Togepi happily hopped across the plank, ignoring Jessie.

Jessie got down on her hands and knees. "I won't stand here and let a rare Pokémon get away so easily," she said. Then her voice turned syrupy-sweet. "Togepi, I'm coming to rescue you!"

Jessie began to slowly crawl across the plank. The wood creaked under her weight.

"Get back here!" James yelled. "You'll fall!"

"You'll get scrambled," Meowth added.

"Stop all that chattering," Jessie said. "I'm almost —"

Crack! The plank splintered underneath her.

Jessie plummeted to the ground below.

"We'll save you!" James cried. He and Meowth ran down the stairs of the building. They held out their arms, ready to catch Jessie as she fell.

Crash! They missed. Jessie landed in a pile of garbage next to them.

James ran up to her. "Jess, are you all right?"

Jessie brushed a banana peel from her face. "Fine, no thanks to you!" she said angrily. "Not only am I stuck in this trash heap, but I lost Togepi, too."

Overhead, Togepi hopped off the roof . . .

. . . and landed on Jessie's head!

Jessie was stunned for a second. Then she quickly grabbed Togepi and grinned.

"You're not getting away this time!" Jessie said. She climbed out of the garbage pile. "We're taking you to the Boss."

Meowth sniffed the air. "Maybe you should take a shower first," the Pokémon said.

Jessie glared at Meowth.

"J-just a suggestion," Meowth said meekly.

Jessie, James, and Meowth walked down the street to the back of Viridian City Gym. A plain black door marked the secret entrance to the gym — for Giovanni's henchmen only.

James punched in the secret code, then led the way down the hall. Two guards stood in front of Giovanni's office.

"We're here to see the Boss," James announced.

"We've got something that he wants," Jessie said.

"The Boss is in the gym," one of the guards said curtly.

The other guard chuckled. "Yeah, he's making mincemeat out of another Pokémon trainer."

Down the hall, a door to the gym opened. Giovanni backed out of the door. "That's what you get for trying to battle my secret weapon!" Giovanni called into the gym. "I possess the ultimate Pokémon. It can never be defeated!"

"What's he talking about?" James whispered to Jessie.

"I don't know," Jessie replied. "But it doesn't matter. The Boss will forget all about his ultimate Pokémon when he sees Togepi."

Giovanni brushed past them and walked into his office.

"You can go in now," the guard said.

Jessie held Togepi behind her back. She wanted the rare Pokémon to be a surprise.

Jessie, James, and Meowth stepped into Giovanni's office. The Boss sat behind a large desk. His stern-looking face looked as though it was chiseled out of concrete. In his lap sat a Persian, a Pokémon that looked like a fancy cat.

"Make it quick," the Boss snapped.

"Sir, we've finally captured a special

Pokémon that we think you will really love," Jessie said eagerly.

"It's even rarer than that Pikachu you want so much," James said.

"And it's a real cutie, too!" Meowth added.

Giovanni glared at the trio. "What are you half-wits talking about?"

"We've brought you a rare and valuable Pokémon," Jessie said. She brought Togepi out from behind her back. "It's Togepi!"

Giovanni stared at the tiny Pokémon with the eggshell on its body. He frowned.

"What exactly does this thing do?" he asked.

Jessie began to fidget nervously. "Uh, what *does* Togepi do?"

"Uh, well . . ." James stammered.

"Good question!" said Meowth.

Jessie plopped Togepi on Giovanni's desk. "It would make a nice paperweight!" she offered.

Giovanni's face turned bright red.

"You fools! You search for months and *this* is all you bring me?" he yelled.

Giovanni slammed his fist down on the desk. Startled, Togepi hopped off the desk and onto the floor.

The Persian slid off Giovanni's lap. Bored, it padded across the floor and nudged open the office door. Then it disappeared into the hallway.

Giovanni was too angry to notice.

"You're total incompetents!" he screamed.

Jessie, James, and Meowth stammered out apologies.

A ringing phone interrupted the din.

Giovanni picked up the phone. "What happened?" He looked concerned. "I'll be right there."

He hung up the phone and looked at

Team Rocket. "There's been a problem with my ultimate Pokémon. I have to go," the Boss said. He sighed. "I have no choice but to leave you three in charge of the gym."

Giovanni reached into his desk. He pulled out three red-and-white Poké Balls. Inside the balls were Pokémon that could be used in battle against Pokémon trainers.

The Boss threw the balls to Jessie, James, and Meowth.

"Use these to protect the gym if necessary," he said. Then he rushed out of the room.

Jessie, James, and Meowth looked at one another in disbelief.

"The three of us . . ." Jessie began.

"In charge . . ." James continued.

"Of the gym?" Meowth finished.

The three Pokémon thieves cheered and jumped up and down.

"That means that we're Gym Leaders!" Jessie said.

The three cheered again.

They were so busy cheering they didn't notice that Togepi had hopped out of the open door.

Togepi had escaped!

3

Trapped!

Meowth noticed first.

"Uh, I think we have a problem," Meowth said.

Jessie and James gave each other a high five.

"What problem?" Jessie asked. "We're Gym Leaders now!"

"That's right!" James said. "Pokémon trainers who want to earn an Earth Badge will have to battle us first. It will be so much fun to watch their puny little Pokémon fail."

Meowth pointed to the open door.

"We have a different kind of problem," Meowth said. "Togepi's gone!"

"Who cares about Togepi?" Jessie said. "The Boss didn't like that pipsqueak anyway."

"But Ash and his friends care about Togepi," Meowth reminded them. "We could use Togepi to get to Pikachu."

James looked thoughtful. "That *would* make the Boss happy," James said.

Jessie agreed. "We'll find it. That walking omelette couldn't have gone too far."

"*Then* we'll get to the gym and start battling!" James said.

Viridian City Gym was a large building. Jessie, James, and Meowth traveled down one empty corridor after another. They couldn't find Togepi anywhere.

"Togepi! We miss you so much!" Jessie called out in her fake, sweet voice.

"We'll help you get back to that little twerp — I mean, Ash," James yelled.

Togi togi.

"I heard something!" Jessie said.

"It sounded like Togepi," James agreed.

23

Meowth bounded around a corner. "I think it's coming from over here."

Jessie and James followed Meowth into a dead-end hallway. The hall ended in a door, which was open just a crack.

"Togepi must have gone through there!" Jessie cried.

James and Meowth followed Jessie through the door onto a staircase leading downward. The old wooden stairs creaked as they stepped on them.

Without warning, the door behind them slammed shut.

Startled, Meowth tripped over a step. The Pokémon hurled into Jessie and

James. The three tumbled down the stairs and landed on the floor below with a thud.

Jessie rubbed her elbow. "Watch it, you clumsy cat!" she snapped.

"*Meowth!* We need some light in here," Meowth said. In the dark it could make out a string hanging from the ceiling. The Pokémon pulled on the string, lighting a dim bulb overhead.

Team Rocket looked around the room. They were in the basement. Storage boxes lined the gray concrete walls. A computer terminal sat in one corner.

Jessie absentmindedly kicked some of the boxes.

"I don't see Togepi anywhere," she moaned.

"This is useless," James said. "Let's get back up to the gym and start being Gym Leaders."

James stomped back up the creaky staircase. He grabbed the doorknob and pulled.

"Just our luck," James said. "It's stuck."

Jessie pushed past him. "Let me handle

25

it, you weakling." She grabbed the doorknob and yanked as hard as she could. The
doorknob came off in her hands!

Jessie kicked at the door with her long
black boots. James pounded the door with
his fists.

It was no use. The door wouldn't open.

"Now you've done it," Meowth said.
"We're trapped!"

4

Team Rocket in Trouble

Jessie spun around. "What do you mean, now *we've* done it?" she asked, her eyes flashing angrily.

"That's right," James said. "You're the one who led us into this dungeon in the first place."

"I was only trying to find Togepi," Meowth protested. "You're the ones who let Togepi escape."

"*Us!*" Jessie yelled. "*You* were supposed to be watching Togepi."

"Actually, Jess," James said, "you were

the last one who had Togepi." He smiled. "So I guess this really *is* all your fault!"

Jessie stomped across the room. "If I hadn't risked my life on top of that roof, we never would have captured Togepi in the first place! Sometimes I don't know what I'm doing with you two cowards."

"Coward? Who are you calling a coward?" James barked at Jessie. The two Pokémon thieves were nose to nose.

"Cut it out!" Meowth yelled. "While you're arguing, Togepi is running around out there. We've got to find a way out of here."

Jessie and James took a step back from each other.

Jessie took a deep breath. "Meowth's right," she said.

James nodded. "But how do we get out?"

Meowth pointed to the computer. "Maybe that can help."

James looked confused. "What are we supposed to do? Play computer games until help arrives?"

Jessie rolled her eyes. "No, you lamebrain. That computer is probably rigged up to the gym's operating system. There might be a floor plan in there. That would show us how to get out."

"Of course," James said sheepishly. "I was just joking."

Jessie ran up to the computer and turned it on. The Team Rocket logo flashed on the screen.

"Here's a menu of all of the files on this computer," Jessie said, pressing a button.

"I don't see anything about a floor plan," James said.

"There's something." Meowth pointed to a file entry on the menu. It read JESSIE, JAMES, AND MEOWTH.

"It's a file about us," Jessie said.

"I can see that," James said. "But why is your name first?"

"Don't worry, James," Jessie said. "They probably just listed us in alphabetical order."

"Oh, right," James said. Then his eyes lit up. "Hey, then that would mean —"

"Stop yammering and let's see what it says!" Meowth said, hitting the Enter key.

Photos of Jessie, James, and Meowth appeared on the screen.

JAMES: WOULD BE CLEVER IF HE WERE NOT STUPENDOUSLY DIM-WITTED.

JESSIE: HAS A GREAT POTENTIAL FOR EVIL, BUT IS TOO SELF-ABSORBED TO USE IT.

MEOWTH: THIS POKÉMON HAS THE AMAZING ABILITY TO SPEAK. UNFORTUNATELY, NOTHING IT SAYS IS WORTH LISTENING TO.

"Do you see that?" Jessie said. "The Boss thinks I have great potential!"

"Well, he thinks I'm stupendous," James said proudly.

"And he called me amazing!" Meowth said, preening its fur.

They kept reading.

AS A TEAM, THESE THREE HAVE MADE SOME OF THE MOST INCRED-IBLE BUNGLES IN THE HISTORY OF THE TEAM ROCKET EMPIRE.

"Wow! He thinks we're an incredible team," Jessie said.

"We are an incredible team, Jess," James said. "We shouldn't fight so much."

"That's right!" Meowth said. "When we put our minds together, we can do anything. In fact, that reminds me of the time we had one of our greatest battles . . ."

A Battle in the Forest

"I'll never forget the day we snuck up on Ash, Misty, and Pikachu in the forest," Meowth began. "Of course, it was *my* amazing tracking ability that got us there in the first place."

"Oh, brother," Jessie said.

Meowth ignored her and continued with the story. "We took Ash and Misty completely by surprise. They were arguing, as always. I still remember the look of fear on their faces when they saw me leap out into the clearing they were standing in.

33

"Pikachu was so close. I could have reached out and grabbed it. But you two numbskulls decided to have a Pokémon battle first.

"Jessie threw her Ekans. This was back in the days before Ekans evolved into Arbok. Ekans looked like a big, purple snake back then.

"James threw his Koffing. Since then, Koffing has evolved into Weezing, a big black poison cloud with two heads. But in those days, Koffing only had one head.

"Even though they hadn't evolved yet, those Pokémon looked pretty frightening. Ash was in a panic. He had never been in a real Pokémon battle before that.

"Ash was also a Goody Two-shoes. You guys broke the rules when you put two Pokémon into battle at the same time. But Ash didn't want to break the rules. He tried to start the battle with Pikachu, but James put a stop to that. He ordered Koffing to do a Sludge Attack. Koffing squirted brown sludge right into Pikachu's eyes. That annoying little lightning mouse couldn't see a thing!

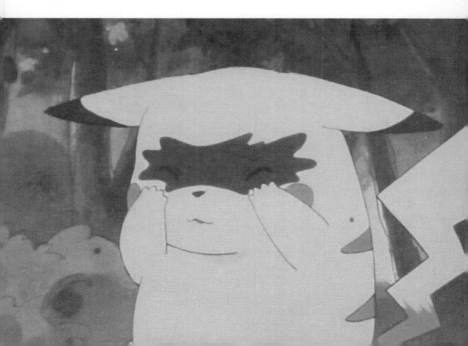

"Ash had no choice. He had to battle with a Pokémon less powerful than Pikachu. He threw a Poké Ball and out came Pidgeotto.

"Ash's Pidgeotto flew through the air with its sturdy wings. James ordered Koffing to do another Sludge Attack. Koffing floated in the air and sent another spray of sludge in Pidgeotto's direction. But Pidgeotto dodged the attack.

"Then Jessie ordered Ekans to take a bite out of Pidgeotto. Ekans stretched its long neck into the air and chomped away. But Pidgeotto dodged Ekans's fangs.

"Ash called for a quick attack. Pidgeotto swooped down on Ekans, its talons bared. But Jessie thought fast. She ordered Ekans to go underground. The snakelike Pokémon burrowed into the dirt before Pidgeotto could hit.

"Pidgeotto was distracted. Koffing snuck up behind it, and spit out poison gas and sludge at Pidgeotto. That brainless bird didn't even know what hit it!

"Pidgeotto was stunned. Then Ekans

burst through the ground and caught Pidgeotto by surprise. Koffing and Ekans slammed into Pidgeotto with all their might. Pidgeotto fainted.

"Ash had to call back Pidgeotto. Pikachu still couldn't see, and Ash only had one Pokémon left — a measly little Caterpie.

"I laughed so hard when that little green Bug Pokémon popped out of Ash's Poké Ball. It looked like Team Rocket had won the battle for sure.

"But even though Ekans and Koffing were strong, they didn't have the brains of a Pokémon like me. You need brawn *and* brains to battle a Pokémon — even a little Caterpie.

"Ash ordered Caterpie to do a String Shot. Caterpie opened its mouth and poured out strands and strands of strong silk. The silk strands covered Ekans and Koffing. They couldn't move! They were out of commission.

"Then it looked like Team Rocket had lost the battle for sure. That's when I stepped in. I showed that puny little bug what a real Pokémon is made of. That creepy critter didn't know what hit it.

"And that," said Meowth proudly, "is how I won the battle against Ash!"

Jessie yanked Meowth's curly tail.

"You nitwit!" Jessie said. "That's not how it happened!"

"That's right," James said. "If I remember correctly, Caterpie had you wrapped up in a cocoon, too. We had to carry you out of the forest. Thanks to you, we lost our chance to get Pikachu."

Meowth blushed. "Um, I guess I forgot about that part."

Jessie got a dreamy look in her eyes. "I'll tell you about a really great battle," Jessie said. "Thanks to me, we had Pikachu right where we wanted it . . ."

6

Fashion Flashback

"It all started with my brilliant plan to open a fashion salon for Pokémon," Jessie remembered. "It was so simple, yet so devious. Pokémon trainers brought their Pokémon to us for magnificent makeovers."

"More like magnificent messes," Meowth said.

"That's just your opinion," Jessie snapped. "Besides, we made a fortune. And we were in the perfect position to steal rare Pokémon. If a trainer brought in a Pokémon worth poaching, all we had to do was distract the trainer, grab the Pokémon, and leave town.

"Things were proceeding just as I planned. We were the hottest salon in town. I knew it would be only a matter of time before we nabbed a rare Pokémon.

"And then one day, our wildest dreams came true. Ash's annoying little friend, Misty, came into the salon with her even more annoying little Pokémon, Psyduck.

"I quickly seized the moment. Misty didn't recognize us in our high-fashion disguises. I knew that if we could get Misty to trust us, she might reveal valuable information that would help us capture Pikachu. So I gave her a fabulous makeover. She loved it. I had her in the palm of my hand."

"Don't forget I was there, too, Jess," James interrupted. "I have a natural flair for fashion, you know."

"Whatever." Jessie ignored him. "Anyway, Misty was about to tell us everything we wanted to know. And then, as usual, Meowth almost ruined everything."

"Hey!" Meowth protested.

Jessie glared at the Pokémon. "Well, it's true! You slipped up and gave away our true identity. Misty tried to run out of the salon when she found out we were really Team Rocket.

"That's when I saved the day — again — with another brilliant idea. I knew Misty would be even more useful to us as bait. So we tied her up in some high-fashion ropes and waited for Ash to fall for our trap.

"We didn't have to wait long. Ash, Brock, and Pikachu burst through the doors of the salon. Behind them was their new friend, Suzy, a Pokémon breeder, and Vulpix, Suzy's favorite Pokémon.

"Ash tried to act tough. He said he wouldn't trade Misty for Pikachu. He and Brock challenged us to a battle instead.

"That was no problem, because I had the foresight to install a battle platform in the salon. I pushed a button, and the beautiful platform rose from the ground. It looked just like a fashion runway. Then it was time for Salon Rocket's fashion extravaganza and Pokémon battlethon to begin!

"I called on Ekans and Koffing. Both

were dressed for the occasion in expensive fashions from Paris. They looked adorable.

"Ash called on Pikachu. Brock called on Geodude, his Rock Pokémon. Geodude made the first move. That blustering boulder flew across the battle platform and

crashed into my
Ekans. But Ekans
was up to the chal-
lenge.

Ekans grabbed
its tail with its
mouth and rolled
like a wheel across
the platform at light-
ning speed and
slammed into
Pikachu with amaz-
ing force — not to mention amazing style.
Pikachu didn't know what hit it.

"Pikachu tried to fight back with a
Thundershock. But the shock was too weak
to do any damage to Ekans and Koffing.
James ordered Koffing to do a Sludge
Attack and, in a flash, Pikachu and
Geodude were covered with sludge. Highly
unfashionable!

"Ekans and Koffing lunged to make their
final attack. There was a minor setback
when they tripped over their outfits. But
they got back up again.

"Pikachu and Geodude couldn't shake the sludge. They had to give up. Victory was ours!" Jessie smiled triumphantly.

James tapped Jessie on the shoulder. "Uh, Jess," James said. "Didn't you forget something? We lost that battle."

"What do you mean?" Jessie said angrily. "It was my greatest triumph."

"I think it was your greatest failure," James said. "Remember, Ash's friend, Suzy called on her Vulpix. That Pokémon may look like an ordinary little fox, but it has big firepower. One Fire Spin from Vulpix sent us blasting off again."

"That's funny," Jessie said. "I don't remember any of that."

"Well, maybe you will remember this," James said. "It's the time I had Pikachu right in my hands!"

7

The End of Team Rocket?

"Your fashion plan was nothing compared to my brilliant plan," James said. "I came up with the idea to hire someone to capture Pikachu for us.

"Meowth read a magazine article about a kid who was great at capturing Pokémon," James continued. "A kid called Snap.

"But like always, Meowth made a mistake. Snap was good at capturing Pokémon — on film. He was a photographer, not a Pokémon trainer. So as usual, we

were stuck in the middle of nowhere —
without Pikachu.

"That's when I got an idea to dig a trap
and capture Pikachu ourselves. We dug a
deep hole in the path and covered it with
soft dirt. We hid behind the bushes and
waited.

"My plan worked like a charm. Ash and
his gang of Goody Two-shoes came walking
down the path, completely unaware that
they were in the presence of pure evil. They
fell into the pit, just as I planned."

Meowth rolled his eyes. "But it didn't go
according to plan!" Meowth protested. "You
dug the pit on top of an old water pipe. The
floor of the pit cracked. Ash and Pikachu
fell into the water pipe, and the water carried them away."

"That was my plan," James replied. "The
water carried Ash and Pikachu to the top of
a waterfall. Snap tried to save them by
throwing his camera strap to Ash. Ash
grabbed on to the camera strap, and
Pikachu hung on to Ash's back. They were

hanging by a thread — just where I wanted them!

"I gave Meowth a Pikachu-proof net with a long handle that I made myself. Meowth reached over and used the net to snatch Pikachu from Ash's back. It was beautiful. We were standing safely on land next to the waterfall. We had Pikachu trapped in the net, right in our very hands. And that twerp Ash was dangling over the waterfall."

James chuckled. "Ash looked like he needed a nice, cool drink of water. So I made it easier for him. I threw him one of my homemade Rocket Bombs. Ash plummeted into the waterfall — and out of our lives forever!"

Jessie smacked James on the back of the head. "You're remembering it all wrong. It was your Rocket Bomb that ruined everything!"

"She's right!" Meowth said. "Ash tricked you. You were holding a Rocket Bomb in your hand. Ash grabbed Snap's camera and asked us to pose for a picture. While we were posing, the bomb was ticking. Then it exploded! It knocked us off our feet."

"But Pikachu was safe, as always," Jessie said. "Snap pulled Ash out of the water. Then Ash sent Bulbasaur to rescue Pikachu. Bulbasaur used a Razor Leaf Attack to cut open the net and set Pikachu free. Then Bulbasaur used a Vine Whip Attack on us!"

Meowth rubbed its tail. "That still smarts!" it said.

"We lost that battle. We lost Pikachu," Jessie said angrily. "And it was all your fault!"

"My fault?" James said. "Well, at least I didn't come up with some stupid plan like opening a fashion salon. How was that supposed to help us get Pikachu?"

"Good point!" Meowth said.

"Shut your big Meowth," Jessie said. "My

plans would work fine if you weren't constantly messing them up."

"Mine, too," James said.

"Well if that's how you feel," Meowth said, "I guess you don't need me at all."

"I don't need either of you!" Jessie said.

"Me either!" James said.

"Then I guess that settles it," Jessie said. "We're all going solo. From this moment on, we'll be evil on our own."

James nodded. "No more Team Rocket!"

8

Memories

"That's fine with me!" Meowth yelled. It turned its back on Jessie and James.

"Me too!" James said. He stormed off into a corner.

"I don't need Team Rocket anyway!" Jessie said. She sat down on a wooden crate and put her face in her hands.

The three former members of Team Rocket quietly fumed.

Jessie's words echoed in her mind. *I don't need Team Rocket anyway,* she thought. *My life was much better before I met James and Meowth.*

Then she sighed. In her heart, she knew it wasn't true. Life before Team Rocket wasn't much fun. She didn't have any toys to play with as a little girl. Not even a tiny Pokémon doll. And to make things worse, she had no friends.

Then she met James, and she wasn't lonely anymore. When they met Meowth, their life of evil really began. Being a high-profile Pokémon poacher was full of glamour and excitement. It was a lot more fun than longing for stupid Pokémon dolls.

But now it's over, Jessie thought sadly.

In his corner of the basement, James thought about his life before Team Rocket, too.

Jess and Meowth are so infuriating, James thought. *But they're not nearly as awful as what's waiting for me back home.*

Home for James was a big, beautiful mansion. James could go home anytime he wanted and live in the lap of luxury. There was only one problem.

James's parents wanted him to get married. And the woman they wanted him to marry was just terrible. Jessebelle never wanted him to have any fun. She'd never let him travel around, striking fear into the hearts of Pokémon trainers everywhere. Jessebelle wanted to change James, wanted him to be something he wasn't-. She was always trying to teach him proper manners and tell him what to do. But Jessie and Meowth were happy with James just the way he was.

Well, most of the time, anyway.

But it's no use now, James thought. *He sighed. I guess I'll have to go home and face my parents — and Jessebelle.*

At the same time, Meowth stared at the cold basement walls. *Jessie and James are always blaming me for everything,* Meowth thought. *They just don't appreciate all the hard work I do for them.*

Meowth remembered the first time it met Jessie and James. Meowth was living in the streets of the big city, when it met a pretty

Pokémon named Meowzy. Meowth's heart was lost. It tried everything it could to impress Meowzy. But nothing worked. Meowzy wanted nothing to do with a grungy street Pokémon.

Then Meowth got an idea. Meowzy thought humans were great. So Meowth did everything it could to become like a human. It learned to walk on two legs. It took speech lessons. After a long time, Meowth finally learned to talk.

Meowth was sure Meowzy would fall in love with it now. But Meowzy didn't. Meowzy fell in love with a lousy Persian instead! After everything Meowth had done.

Meowzy deserted Meowth. All of the other Pokémon thought Meowth was a freak. But not Jessie and James. They rescued Meowth from the big city. They let Meowth join their team. And they never made Meowth feel like a grungy gutter cat the way Meowzy had.

Those guys stuck by me, Meowth thought. *I can't leave them now.*

Meowth turned around and cleared its throat. "Uh, guys, I was thinking . . ."

Jessie jumped up and hugged Meowth. "You don't have to say it. I feel the same way."

"If you guys are talking about getting Team Rocket back together again, then

count me in!" James said. He hugged Jessie and Meowth.

Team Rocket hugged one another and sobbed happily. Then Jessie jumped back.

"Yuck! You two are as sappy as that silly Ash," she said.

"Speaking of Ash, isn't that his voice?" James said.

From outside the gym, they could hear Ash calling for Togepi.

"*Meowth!* Ash is right outside!" Meowth cried.

"He's bound to come to the gym looking for a challenge," Jessie said.

"And as Gym Leaders, we will battle him," James said.

"And steal Pikachu!" Meowth said happily. "But we've got to get out of this basement first."

"Looks like it's time for another brilliant Team Rocket plan," James added.

Jessie ran to the computer. "We've got to stop jabbering and figure this out," she said.

Jessie pushed some buttons on the keyboard. A floor plan of the gym popped up on the screen.

"According to this map, there is another door in the basement," James said. "It's right . . ."

James looked up. Next to the computer screen was a wooden door marked EXIT.

". . . here," James finished weakly.

"It was there all along!" Meowth said.

"It doesn't matter now," Jessie said. She stared at the screen, her eyes gleaming. "This floor plan is interesting. With a few minor adjustments, I think we can rig up the gym so that Ash will lose for sure!"

"A booby-trapped gym!" James said. "Oh, Jess, you're so clever."

"Let's get down to business," Meowth said. "If we work together, we can't be beat."

"And soon . . ." Jessie said.

". . . Pikachu will be ours!" James cried.

9

challenge in Viridian city Gym

In the basement of Viridian City Gym, Jessie, James, and Meowth worked on their devious plan.

Meanwhile, outside the gym, Ash, Brock, Misty, and Pikachu still searched for Togepi.

"There's no sign of Togepi anywhere," Brock said.

Misty glared at Ash. "If anything happens to Togepi, I'll never forgive you!" she said.

Ash was downcast. "Togepi will turn up somewhere," he said half-heartedly.

"*Pi pi pi!*" Pikachu called out.

A tiny voice responded.

"*Togi togi!*"

"That sound is coming from behind the gym doors!" Ash cried. He and his friends ran to the gym entrance. The guards were gone. They quickly pulled open the heavy doors.

Togepi was right behind the doors. It chirped and flapped its arms happily when it saw its friends.

Misty scooped up Togepi in her arms. "Thank goodness you're safe!" she said.

But Brock had a look of concern on his face. "Something's not right," he said. "It's too quiet in here. Isn't Gary supposed to be having a Pokémon battle?"

Ash, Misty, and Pikachu peered inside the darkened gym. There were figures sprawled out on the gym floor.

Ash ran up to one of them. It was Gary!

Brock and Misty ran to Gary's cheerleaders. They were lying dazed on the floor, as though they had been stunned.

"Gary, are you all right?" Ash lifted up Gary's head.

Gary opened his eyes.

"Gary, what happened here?" Ash asked.

Gary spoke slowly. "A Pokémon that we've never seen before did this," Gary said. "It had powers that I've never encountered in my life."

"That's impossible," Brock said.

Gary shook his head. "No, it's true. There's something strange going on in this gym. It's like there's an evil force running this place. A force like —"

"Team Rocket!" Misty called out.

Ash spun around. The gym lights flashed on all at once. Jessie and James stepped into the room and onto a low, red platform at the other end of the gym.

"Prepare for trouble," Jessie said.

"And make it double," James finished.

Jessie and James began to recite their motto:

"To protect the world from devastation,
To unite all peoples within our nation.
To denounce the evils of truth and love.
To extend our reach to the stars above . . ."

"Oh no, it's them!" Ash moaned.

66

"Again!" Brock and Misty added.

Jessie scowled. "Why do you little twerps always interrupt us before we get to finish?" she complained.

"We know what you're going to say," Misty responded. "It's never any different!"

Jessie smiled smugly. "Ah, but today is very different."

"Something's happened that's going to make you very jealous!" James said.

A glittering ball descended from the ceiling of the gym. The ball opened, and Meowth fell out in a shower of confetti. The confetti — and Meowth — landed on Jessie and James.

"Let's celebrate!" Meowth said. "We just got a big promotion."

"That's right, " James said. "The three of us are the new leaders of this gym!"

The news stunned Ash, Brock, and Misty.

"You guys are Gym Leaders?" Ash said in disbelief.

Jessie nodded. "That's right," she said. "The Boss put us in charge of the gym a little while ago. He had to leave on an emergency."

"I bet it had something to do with that strange Pokémon," Gary guessed.

Jessie continued. "Not only are we in charge of the gym, but we're in charge of the

Earth Badge!"
She held out
the glittering
green stone.

"The Boss?
The Earth
Badge?" Ash
said. "You
mean this
gym is con-
trolled by Team Rocket?"

"That's right," James said. "Our Boss runs this gym. And now we're the boss of you! If you want an Earth Badge, you'll have to defeat us."

Ash stepped forward. "That's just what I'm going to do!" he said.

Jessie laughed. "Then step right into the ring we've prepared for you."

Jessie pressed a button on the rail that surrounded the platform. The red platform began to rise into the air. Soon Jessie was standing fifteen feet above the ground.

At the same time, a blue platform began to rise up next to Ash.

"Don't get in, Ash," Misty warned. "It's a trick."

"They must have booby-trapped it somehow!" Brock said.

James sneered. "If you run away now, you won't get your Earth Badge," he said.

"I'm not running anywhere!" Ash said. He climbed up a ladder on the back of the platform. He stood high above the gym floor, facing Jessie across the gym.

"What do you say we begin with three Pokémon each, no time limit?" Jessie suggested.

"Fine," Ash said. He grabbed one of the Poké Balls on his belt. "Let's battle!"

Jessie threw out the three Poké Balls that the Boss had given her.

Flash! Machamp appeared. This gray Rock Pokémon had four strong arms.

Flash! Kingler

appeared. This orange Water Pokémon looked like a giant crab with sharp claws.

Flash!

Rhydon appeared. This tough-looking Pokémon looked like a rhinoceros that walked on two legs. It had a long, sharp horn on the end of its nose.

Jessie smiled, pleased. "This should be a cinch."

"And don't forget our secret weapons!" Meowth whispered loudly.

"Be careful," Brock called up to Ash. "They're up to something."

"Right," Ash said. "But first, I need to choose a Pokémon."

Ash threw a Pokémon into the air.

"Squirtle!" Ash cried. "I choose you!"

Squirtle appeared in a flash of light. This Water Pokémon looked like a cute, harmless turtle, but Ash had trained it well. Squirtle really knew how to fight.

Jessie just laughed. "Squirtle? Is that the best you can do?" She pointed at Machamp. "Machamp! Karate Chop!" she commanded.

Machamp rushed at Squirtle and began delivering karate-style punches with its strong arms.

Squirtle grunted from the impact. At the same time, Ash felt a sharp shock tear through his body. His platform lit up with electric light.

Ash groaned and grabbed the railing in front of him. He could barely stand.

"What's happening?" Misty asked.

James smiled. "That's one of the custom features here in our gym," he explained. "In that box, the trainer feels all the pain his or her Pokémon feels!"

10

The Battle Heats Up

"Do you want to quit now, twerp?" Jessie asked.

Ash shook his head. "Never," he said weakly.

Gary called up to Ash. "Try another Pokémon, Ash," Gary suggested. "Squirtle can't beat Machamp. It's too powerful."

Ash nodded. He threw another Poké Ball out into the battle arena.

"Bulbasaur! Go!"

A Grass Pokémon appeared. Bulbasaur

looked like a small dinosaur with a plant bulb on its back.

Jessie frowned. "Then I'll choose Kingler!"

Kingler and Bulbasaur ran toward each other and faced off in the center of the gym floor.

"Bulbasaur! Vine Whip!"

The plant bulb on Bulbasaur's back opened up. Four strong, green vines lashed out at Kingler.

"Kingler! Harden!" Jessie commanded.

A hard shield formed around Kingler's body. The vines crashed against the shield, but they couldn't do any damage.

"Kingler! Bubblebeam!" Jessie yelled.

Bubbles streamed out of Kingler's mouth. The

rock-hard bubbles slammed into Bulbasaur.

"Owwwwww!" Ash yelled. Each time a bubble hit Bulbasaur, a jolt of pain coursed through his body. He fell to his knees.

"Ash, you can't win!" Gary said. "These Pokémon are too strong."

James and Meowth jumped up and down. "We're going to win! We're going to win!" they shouted.

But Ash slowly rose to his feet. He had a determined look on his face.

"I won't give up," Ash said. "I've come too far to quit now. I trust my Pokémon."

Ash held out another Poké Ball. "We can do it!"

Gary looked at Ash. "Maybe he can," he said with admiration.

Ash threw the Poké Ball.

"Pidgeotto! Quick Attack!" he yelled.

Pidgeotto burst out of the Poké Ball. The birdlike Pokémon flew through the air, straight at Rhydon. It used its beak to land a hard blow on Rhydon's chest.

At the same time, an electric shock shot

through the red platform and made Jessie's feet tingle. She gasped in surprise.

"Pidgeotto! Double-Edge Attack!" Ash commanded.

Pidgeotto slammed into Rhydon again and again with its sharp beak and powerful wings. The blows came too quickly for Rhydon to react.

On the red platform, Jessie screamed as an electric shock zapped her.

"James, why did you set it to give shocks on both sides?" she yelled down.

James shrugged. "I didn't think it would matter," he said. "I never thought we would lose!"

"Well, turn it off!" Jessie screamed.

James looked panicky. "I don't know how!"

Meowth pulled out a small control box from behind its back. The box had one red button and one blue button.

"Don't worry, James," Meowth said. "Luckily, I made this little gadget in case we did lose. All you have to do is hit the blue button, and good-bye competition!"

Meowth put a finger on the blue button.
Gary ran up to Meowth.

"Oh, no you don't!" he cried.

Gary tackled Meowth. The control box skidded across the floor.

Gary and Meowth were about to fight. But they quickly stopped at the sound of Jessie's voice.

"Team Rocket is not about to lose this match!" she yelled. "We can do anything together, right guys?"

"Right!" Meowth and James said.

Jessie took two Poké Balls from her belt.

"All Pokémon attack at once!" she cried. She threw the Poké Balls. "Go Arbok! Go Weezing!"

Two more Pokémon appeared on the gym floor. Arbok hissed. Weezing floated in the air.

"You can't use new Pokémon now," Misty protested. "It's against the rules!"

"I make the rules for this gym," Jessie said.

"Well, if those are the rules, then I can use

a new Pokémon, too," Ash said. "Go, Pikachu!"

Pikachu ran out into the battle arena. With a leap, it hopped up on Arbok's back. Pikachu released a big electric charge from its body. The yellow light electrified Arbok. Then the beams of electricity shot out and zapped Weezing.

Up on the red platform, Jessie screamed as the electricity shocked her, too.

Pikachu's powerful charge zoomed across the gym floor. Machamp, Kingler, and Rhydon got a taste of Pikachu's amazing lightning powers. They collapsed to the floor in a heap.

Ash let out a cheer. "We did it!" Ash yelled. "We won the match!"

11

Team Rocket's Secret Weapon

Gary's cheerleaders let out a cheer for Ash.

"He's the winner! He's our Ash!
Let's all have a victory bash!
He's the victor! He's our man!
No one wins like Ketchum can!"

Ash climbed down from the platform.

Squirtle, Bulbasaur, Pidgeotto, and Pikachu ran up to Ash. He hugged them all.

"You all did great," Ash said. "I'm so proud of you."

James and Meowth climbed up the platform to help Jessie. She was sprawled out on the floor. Arbok and Weezing lay motionless next to her.

"Jessie, can you hear me?" James asked worriedly.

"Can you move?" asked Meowth.

Jessie sat up. "I'm lucky I can breathe after what you did to me! Why did I get the shocks? What kind of stupid plan was that you came up with?"

"But Jess," James said, "I thought we were a team, remember? We all came up with that plan."

Jessie stood up and faced James. "Don't you dare try to blame me —"

"Hey Jessie!" Ash called out.

Jessie and James stopped arguing.

"I won the match fair and square," Ash said. "And now I want the Earth Badge that I earned."

Jessie grinned evilly. She held out the badge. "Well, you're not getting it!" she taunted.

"Hey! That's cheating," Ash said.

"Well, I'm a cheater!" Jessie said.

"Brilliant, Jess," James said. "We've got something Ash wants. And Ash has something we want. Maybe we can get Pikachu for the Boss after all."

"We really are a great team," Meowth said. Then Meowth froze.

"Togi togi."

Meowth looked down. Togepi had hopped over to the control box on the floor. It had one tiny hand on top of the red button.

"Stop!" Meowth yelled. "Get away from that thing!"

"What's going on?" Jessie and James asked.

"Well, the blue button blows up Ash's platform," Meowth said. "And the red button blows up —"

Togepi pressed the red button.

"— our platform!" Meowth cried.

An explosion rocked the platform's base. Billowing clouds of black smoke filled the air. The platform rose out of the floor like a rocket ship.

"It looks like Team Rocket is blasting off again!" yelled Jessie, James, and Meowth.

The platform shot through the roof of the gym. The Earth Badge flew out of Jessie's hands. It dropped to the gym floor below.

And landed right in Ash's palm.

"I finally got my Earth Badge!" Ash said proudly.

High above, Team Rocket floated through the clouds.

"It looks like Team Rocket goofed again," James said. "Maybe the Boss is right about us."

"Don't be a fool, James," Jessie said. "We had Ash right where we wanted him. We've never been so close to defeating that twerp before. And you know what that means . . ."

James brightened. "It means that *next* time, we'll get Pikachu for sure!"

Coming Soon . . .

POKÉMON #6

Charizard, Go!

It is the biggest Pokémon battle of Ash's life. And he doesn't want to lose. Fire fights Fire but can Ash trust Charizard to fight for him? Ash raised Charizard from a stray Charmander — but Charizard is stubborn and never listens to Ash. When the competition heats up, will Charizard come through for Ash?

Catch It in February!

About the Author

Tracy West has been writing books for more than ten years. When she's not playing the blue version of the Pokémon game (she started with a Squirtle), she enjoys reading comic books, watching cartoons, and taking long walks in the woods (looking for wild Pokémon). She lives in a small town in New York with her family and pets.

POKÉMON

GOTTA CATCH 'EM ALL!